Wendy and the Bullies

by NANCY K. ROBINSON

Illustrated by INGRID FETZ

SCHOLASTIC BOOK SERVICES
NEW YORK • TORONTO • LONDON • AUCKLAND • SYDNEY • TOKYO

ISBN 0-590-30161-6

12 11 10 9 8 7 6 5 4 3 2 1   2   0 1 2 3 4 5/8

This book is dedicated with love to Kenneth, Alice and Jessica.

Stanley

"Ver-r-ry nice," said Mrs. Dover, the art teacher.

She was standing behind Wendy, looking at the painting on Wendy's easel. Wendy liked it, too. It was a painting of a mother and two children visiting a museum. They were all holding hands and looking at tiny paintings on the wall. Wendy was proud that each tiny painting was a perfect little picture in itself.

But Wendy didn't like Mrs. Dover saying, "Ver-r-ry nice." Everyone would notice her.

Sure enough. As soon as Mrs. Dover moved on, Stanley Kane, who was painting at the next easel, said, "Ver-r-r-ry nice," in a high, cracked voice. Wendy pretended not to hear. She went to the supply table to look for a smaller brush.

When she got back, she saw that the children in her painting looked different. The reason they looked different was that they each had a high bushy tail.

"Ver-r-ry nice, ver-r-ry nice," whispered Stanley Kane, not even looking at her. He pretended to be working very hard on his own painting.

Wendy felt her eyes fill up with tears. She hoped they wouldn't roll down her cheeks. She didn't want to rub them, but they burned. Stanley noticed right away.

"Cry baby, cry baby, stick your finger in your eye — baby. . . ," he sang softly.

It was hard to fix up the tails in the painting. Wendy tried to cover them with white paint, but the brown paint was wet so it just made two smudges. Finally she had to make the whole background muddy brown so that the children's bushy tails would blend in. The painting looked awful.

Mrs. Dover came around again. When she saw Wendy's painting, she looked disappointed. She didn't say anything and went back to her desk.

Wendy wanted to tell her what happened, but she couldn't. She couldn't tell anyone but Karen.

At recess Wendy looked all over for Karen. Karen was in the other third-grade class. Wendy waited by the monkey bars where she met Karen every day, but Karen never came.

"She's sick," Linda told her. "You should see what happened to her. She's got a terrible rash. She's all blown up like a balloon. Her mother said she's allergic to seafood." Linda lived across the street from Karen.

"She'll be out all week," Linda said.

Wendy felt lost. She tried to stay close to Linda and her friends, but they went off to play kickball. They didn't ask Wendy to join them.

Then she saw Stanley Kane heading toward her. She looked around for the teacher.

Stanley kept coming toward her. Without stopping, he put out his arm and gave her a hard push. Wendy fell backwards. Her head hit the root of a tree.

She lay there a few seconds, stunned. She heard him hiss at her, "If you say a single thing, you'll be sorry."

Wendy wondered if she were dead. Her head was ringing. She didn't move for a few minutes.

When she sat up, her head was still ringing. Slowly, she walked over to the teacher.

Miss Hunter was busy talking to the other third-grade teacher.

"What is it, Wendy?"

Wendy's mouth was dry. Her voice came out in a small whisper. "I don't feel well. My head hurts."

"I'm sorry to hear that." Miss Hunter

felt Wendy's head. "You'll have to go see the nurse," she said.

The nurse called Wendy's mother on the telephone. Luckily, her mother was at home. She said she would pick up Wendy in ten minutes.

Wendy waited in the nurse's office. She was feeling better, but she'd have to think of something. Somehow she had to be sick until the end of the week.

She would have to be sick until Karen came back to school.

Karen

Karen was Wendy's best friend. She was Wendy's only friend. She was the only one Wendy could talk to.

Karen was afraid of more things than anyone Wendy knew. That made it easier for Wendy to tell Karen about Stanley Kane and all the people she was afraid of.

Karen wasn't just afraid of bullies. She was afraid of the dark. She was afraid of all animals, especially worms. She didn't like to go to the beach because she was afraid of the water. She was afraid of the sand, too. There might be sand crabs.

There was another thing Karen was afraid of. She was afraid of old people. Wendy had trouble understanding that.

"What about your grandmother?" she once asked Karen.

"Ugh!" said Karen, and she shivered.

When they walked home from school, Wendy picked the safest way to walk. Wendy watched out for bullies and Karen watched out for old people.

If an old lady came toward them, Karen would freeze and beg Wendy to cross the street with her. She would clutch Wendy until the old lady was out of sight.

Karen was the only one in the world who knew about Wendy's War Room.

The War Room, officially known as the "STRATEGIC WAR ROOM: Bully Command Post," was in a closet in the basement of Wendy's house. The War Room had been in operation ever since Wendy found out that Stanley Kane was in her class this year. Stanley Kane seemed to pick on her more than on anyone else. Wendy was beginning to feel the whole bully problem was getting out of hand.

Last Friday afternoon Wendy and Karen had an emergency meeting. That was the day Stanley had stuck out his foot and tripped Wendy while she was passing out new workbooks for Miss Hunter.

"This time he has gone too far," whispered Karen. She was holding Wendy's arm tightly as they crawled under the heavy black clothing bags and into the dark closet that smelled of mothballs.

"Shhh. . . ," said Wendy. She shined her flashlight over the wall.

A large map was pinned to the wall. It was a map of the neighborhood with every street carefully drawn. Little push pins marked the spots where bullies might be hanging around.

There were red, orange, and yellow push pins on the map. A red push pin stood for a TYPE A Bully and an orange pin for a TYPE B Bully.

A TYPE B Bully might tease you, play tricks on you, and take things from you, but TYPE A Bullies were really dangerous. They could hurt you.

The yellow pins marked the hangouts of TYPE C Bullies, like Skippy and Tee-jay, who lived around the corner. They could always be counted on to put ice down Wendy's blouse in the winter and worms down her dress in the summer. The big difference between them and TYPE B Bullies was that TYPE C Bullies were smaller than Wendy.

Wendy shined her flashlight on Karen's face. Karen's eyes were opened wide.

"This meeting will now come to order," said Wendy. "Raise your right hand."

Karen held up her hand and repeated the secret oath.

"I do solemnly swear never to tell anyone about the STRATEGIC WAR ROOM: Bully Command Post — even under torture."

". . . and death," added Wendy.

"Do I have to say that?" asked Karen.

"Sounds better," said Wendy.

". . . and death," said Karen. She took a vanilla creme cookie out of a small bag and began to nibble it.

Wendy reached behind an old

suitcase and pulled out the Bully Log Book, a large black notebook carefully arranged into sections.

She turned to a section called INCIDENTS, and read aloud the last entry from the day before.

Date: Oct. 10

Time: 3:15 p.m.

Incident: Micky Lorry stops me, Wendy Kent, outside of school.

Lorry: "Come here kid"
Me: (scared) "What"?
Lorry: (Pushes me against fence)
Lorry: "Got any money"
Me: " Here" (I gave him a quarter)

Lorry! (Gruff voice looking very mean)
"What else have you got?"
(He opens my school bag and throws my books and papers on the sidewalk Finally he desides to take my good eraser, the green one).

In another section, bullies were listed in alphabetical order with their height, weight, age, and habits carefully noted.

There was a section called "Bully Theory or General Observations on Bully Behavior." Here Wendy had written:

"Most bullies travel alone and hardly have any friends, except Mickey Lorry, who gets little kids to work for him by scaring them. Many bullies have a bad family life, but it is hard to feel sorry for them."

Wendy and Karen discussed Stanley Kane and the tripping incident.

"This calls for serious action," said Karen. "You could have really been hurt."

They checked back in the Bully Log Book. Every single day Stanley had done something mean to Wendy.

"A-hem," said Wendy. "I think the time has come to promote Stanley Kane from a TYPE B to a TYPE A Bully."

"I second the motion," said Karen. She held the flashlight while Wendy changed the orange pin on the map to a

red pin. Stanley was now a TYPE A
Bully.

"I'll drink to that," Karen said and ate
another vanilla creme cookie.

Karen was a good listener. The stories
made her furious. The funny thing was
that bullies didn't seem to pick on
Karen. Wendy wondered if it was
because Karen was so little and pretty.
Karen had pale skin with tiny freckles
and long, thick black braids tied with
colored ribbons.

When Wendy finished a story, Karen
would say, "What I'd like to do to him!"

"What?" Wendy would ask, pleased.

"I'd like to hang him upside down
from a tree and throw rotten eggs at
him. They'd hit him in the face and
drip into his eyes and ears."

"What else?" asked Wendy.

"I'd like to be a queen and throw him
off a tower onto sharp pikes. And he
would stick onto these pikes and scream
for help, while I sat on a beautiful

balcony sipping tea and eating ladyfingers."

For someone who was scared of so many things, Karen could think of better punishments than anyone Wendy knew.

But Wendy had her favorite Bully Revenge Story:

"I would be walking along with my trusty dog, Shep." (Wendy didn't have a dog, but her "trusty dog, Shep" was in all of her stories.)

"Stanley Kane would come along and start to tease me, not knowing that Shep is a highly trained attack dog. I wouldn't even look at Stanley, but I would crook my little finger, which is a signal to Shep to take care of Stanley. Shep would grab Stanley by the collar and drag him off into the bushes — Shep knows I don't like to see blood. When Shep is finished with Stanley, we'd go off and get a chocolate ice cream cone for me and a biscuit for

Shep. Then the sanitation truck would come and clean up the street by sticking Stanley into the machine that grinds up garbage."

Next Wendy and Karen discussed what Wendy called "strategy." "Strategy" meant trying to get home from school without bumping into any bullies. Strategy usually meant running for two blocks until they passed Stanley Kane's house. Since Stanley usually fooled around outside of school for a few minutes, they passed his house before he even started home from school.

But then there was Mickey Lorry and his gang to worry about. Wendy and Karen took some back streets and scrambled up a hill which took them through the woods. Then they crawled through the bushes in back of the tennis courts and ran up the street behind Karen's house. They cut through Mrs. Scott's driveway and through the hedges into Karen's backyard.

They couldn't go by way of the front of Karen's house. That was because one of the worst TYPE A Bullies lived right next door to Karen.

Pat Haggerty was two years older than Wendy and Karen and had a very fresh mouth. Worse than that, she could throw very straight. She sat on the porch of her house dangling her feet over the railing. From there, Pat had a good view of the block and just waited for someone to pick on.

A high hedge separated Karen's house from Pat's house. One time Wendy and Karen got into a yelling fight with Pat through the hedge.

"Sticks and stones will break my bones, but names will never harm me," sang Wendy for the twentieth time.

A stone came flying through the hedge and hit Wendy on the head. Her head bled a lot, but Dr. Rosen said it wasn't serious.

"Scalps bleed a lot," said Dr. Rosen.

Wendy's mother called Pat's mother and got mad. That was the last time Wendy told her mother anything.

For days after that, Pat followed Wendy whenever she left Karen's house, calling her "Tattletale" and "Little Rat Kid" all the way home. Sometimes Pat rode a bicycle back and forth in front of Wendy, cutting her off. Once Wendy fell into the bike and scraped the inside of her leg on the fender, but she didn't tell her mother how it happened.

For the next few weeks Karen walked Wendy to her house first, even though it was farther from school. That was the kind of friend Karen was.

Now Karen was sick and Wendy would not go back to school — not for anything!

Wendy's Rare Disease

Wendy sat in the waiting room of Dr. Rosen's office. Her mother sat next to her on the couch flipping pages of a magazine called *Your Baby.*

Wendy had to think fast. A headache wasn't enough to keep her out of school until the end of the week. She tried to cough.

"A-hem, a-hem," she coughed weakly. That was no good.

If only she had a rash or a high fever.

The trouble was she felt perfectly fine. Her head didn't even hurt anymore. So she thought very hard about Stanley. Then she thought about walking home without Karen and bumping into every bully on the map. She started to feel sick.

"I have a rare disease, all right," she said to herself. "I have bully-itis."

"Mom," she said aloud.

"Yes, dear."

"I don't feel well. I feel like throwing up."

She went to the little bathroom off the waiting room. Once she got inside, she felt fine again. So she stuck her finger down her throat, thought very hard about Stanley Kane, and threw up.

While she washed up, she looked in the mirror. Her straight blond hair was all stringy and matted. Her bright green eyes were now dull and glazed. Her face was white in some places and green in others. Wendy was very pleased.

But Dr. Rosen didn't seem worried about her at all. After she got undressed, he took her temperature.

"Normal," he said in his loud, cheerful voice.

He felt her stomach, looked in her ears and down her throat.

"I just threw up," said Wendy.

"Do you feel better now?"

"No," said Wendy.

"Well, if she feels better tomorrow, she can go to school," Dr. Rosen said to Wendy's mother.

Wendy shuddered. "Oh, no," she felt like screaming.

Then she tried coughing again, but Dr. Rosen didn't even seem to notice. He was writing something.

"How are things at school, Wendy?" he asked in his jolly voice.

"Oh, fine," said Wendy and tried to make herself faint by thinking about Stanley again. She gave up trying.

Wendy sat in the car while her mother got some groceries. She thought of ways to break her arm or her leg. She wondered if she had caught something from the children playing in the waiting room of Dr. Rosen's office. Her mother said that was the best way of catching *something*.

"I got your favorite dinner," her

mother said, piling groceries in the back seat of the car. "But I guess you'd better just have soup."

Was her mother testing her to see if she was really sick?

"Soup's okay," said Wendy in her weakest voice, trying to peek in at the groceries.

"Roast beef, baked potatoes, chocolate cake," her mother said.

Wendy gulped. "I just feel like soup."

When Wendy got home, she put on a clean nightgown. She crawled into bed and pulled the covers up to her eyes. She looked at the ceiling and at the blue violets on her wallpaper.

"If only I could stay in bed forever."

Wendy Listens In

Wendy lay in bed watching it get dark outside. Her stuffed animals were lined up on either side of her in her bed. There were 14 stuffed dogs of different sizes, but she couldn't leave any out. They might get hurt feelings. It was a little uncomfortable.

Sometimes it was very uncomfortable when she would roll over and find herself lying on top of the winding key to the music box inside her stuffed poodle. She took turns; each dog got to sleep right next to her once a week.

Wendy's mother came up with a tray.

On the tray there was a small bowl of chicken soup, Jello, and two crackers. Meanwhile, the smell of roast beef cooking downstairs was driving Wendy crazy.

Her mother felt her head.

"Do you feel any better?" she asked.

"I feel dizzy," said Wendy.

"Maybe you should stay home tomorrow," her mother said.

Wendy's father got home late. He came right upstairs to see Wendy. When he walked in, he looked so big and nice, Wendy wanted to jump out of bed and hug him.

He sat at the foot of her bed and squeezed her foot. He looked so sorry for her, Wendy wanted to tell him she really felt okay. But, instead, she coughed. She had found out that the more she coughed, the more she felt like coughing. And the more she coughed, the more it sounded like real coughing.

"Well, how do you feel, lamb chop?" "Lamb chop" was her father's favorite nickname for Wendy. He wiggled her foot and smiled at her and at the 14 stuffed dogs on her pillow.

"Are you going to be better for your birthday?"

"My what?" Wendy usually counted the days to her birthday starting in September. (Her birthday was October 20.) But she must have been so busy keeping track of TYPE A and TYPE B bullies, she forgot all about it.

"This Sunday," her father said. "There is still time if you want to plan a party."

Wendy thought about her one and only friend, Karen.

"No, thank you. I don't feel like a party this year."

Her father looked at her. He seemed worried. He kissed her and whispered,

"I know what will cure you."

"What?" asked Wendy.

"Your birthday present," he laughed.

Wendy didn't even ask what it was. There was only one thing in the world she wanted. She was afraid to ask in case she got disappointed.

"You'll see," her father whispered and

gave her a big hug. Then Wendy made him kiss all 14 stuffed dogs.

When he went downstairs to dinner, Wendy felt terrible. Her parents were so nice to her. They were so worried about her, and here she was tricking them — pretending to be sick. Wendy began to cry softly.

The light was out, but Wendy couldn't sleep. All she could think about was how hungry she was. She could hear the clinking of forks and knives downstairs. Roast beef, gravy, chocolate cake . . . Wendy heard her parents talking, but she couldn't hear what they were saying.

She got out of bed and tiptoed to the top of the stairs. Now she could hear what they were saying.

"I don't think there's a thing wrong with her," her mother said.

Wendy started to shiver.

"But there is something the matter,"

her mother went on. "She's been so quiet lately. When I met Miss Hunter at the first PTA meeting, she said Wendy never talks in class. Even when she is called on, her voice is so low, Miss Hunter always has to ask her to repeat herself. Wendy seems scared a lot of the time and she hardly ever goes outside. Last weekend she stayed inside the whole time."

Her mother wasn't dumb.

"Do you think we should make her go to school?" her father asked.

Wendy held her breath. But now all she could hear was the clattering of dishes. They were clearing the table. The water was running in the kitchen. Wendy figured both her parents were in there. She couldn't hear a thing.

Then they started talking again in the dining room. Wendy's mouth watered. They were eating the chocolate cake now, she guessed.

"That will cheer her up, if anything will," her father was saying.

"What will cheer me up?" Wendy wondered.

The stairs under her feet creaked. Wendy waited, but no one seemed to hear.

"Umm," her mother said. "After I looked in the Bide-a-Wee home, I decided the newspaper ad was our best bet."

"We'll have to get it shots right away."

Wendy nearly tumbled down the stairs. She couldn't believe it. Her dream was coming true. She was getting a dog.

She crept back to her bedroom and put all the stuffed dogs on a shelf. She climbed into bed.

"Good old trusty Shep," she said over and over.

"Good old trusty Shep. He'll show them!"

Enter Shep

Shep arrived Thursday evening after dinner.

The first thing good old trusty Shep said was, "Yip."

He didn't say, "Ruff," or "Bow Wow," or even, "Yap."

Wendy nearly died. She sat in bed and stared at the basket on her bed.

Inside the white wicker basket was a big soft satin pillow. And scrambling around on top of the pillow was a little golden cocker spaniel. He wasn't even as big as a loaf of bread.

"Yip," he said, wagging his whole backside. His legs kept slipping out from under him as he slid around on the satin pillow. He was mostly ears — long, smooth ears with little golden ringlets on them. His big brown eyes took up most of the space on his face.

"Some attack dog," thought Wendy, but she couldn't keep the grin off her face. Her parents were standing next to her bed. They were smiling, too.

Wendy picked Shep up. He didn't seem to have any bones at all. He was warm and silky, and wiggled all over the place. He kept trying to scramble up her neck and snuggle under her hair. He kept licking her the whole time.

"He'll wet the bed," her mother said.

"Just let him stay a minute," her father said.

Shep's heart was beating very fast. Wendy could feel it against her own heart. It made her feel so happy.

"It's okay, Shep," she said over and over. He rolled off and tried walking on the bed. But his paws kept sinking down. He looked very surprised.

"We shouldn't let him get used to walking all over the bed," Wendy's mother said.

"Now, Dorothy, just this once," her father said.

Shep put his paw on Wendy's stomach. When it didn't sink, he crawled onto Wendy again.

"We'll have to keep him in the pantry at night until he is house-trained," her mother said.

They took Shep downstairs. First Wendy tried to let Shep walk down by himself. He flopped down three steps to the landing, tripping on his long ears. Then he just stood, looking down at the long flight of stairs. He put out one paw, and pulled it back.

Wendy laughed. "He's too little to even go down the stairs." She picked him up and carried him down in her arms.

Wendy brought down her oldest stuffed dog and gave it to Shep to play with.

Shep sniffed the stuffed dog. Then he

pushed it with his nose and waited. When it didn't move, he crouched down and got ready to leap.

Wendy giggled. "Go to it, boy. Sic 'em, trusty old Shep."

Shep was chewing on the dog's head furiously, but, when Wendy spoke, he dropped the dog and jumped up to lick her face.

"You don't seem to be the answer to the Bully Problem, Shep," she whispered. "We'll need a whole pack of huskies to protect us."

She sat on the floor and cuddled Shep. "But I love you," she said fiercely into the long, golden ear.

"Going to school tomorrow?" her mother asked.

"Uh — oh — sure, Mom," Wendy answered.

Friday Morning

Wendy got up early the next morning and put on her yellow plaid skirt and vest. She combed her straight blond hair so quickly, she pulled out a handful of hair.

"Ouch!"

Then she ran downstairs to see Shep. Shep was fast asleep, curled around Wendy's stuffed dog. She kissed him on the forehead and went into the kitchen.

Her mother was frying eggs. "I'll have to write a note to your teacher. What should I say?"

"What do you mean?" Wendy was surprised. "Just say I was sick." Wendy had managed to stay out of school for three days. Today was Friday.

"Just say I had the flu. I threw up — you remember."

"No, you didn't have the flu," her mother said slowly. She turned around and studied Wendy. "Darling . . ." she began.

Wendy knew what her mother was going to say next. "Is there anything wrong, dear?" So Wendy changed the subject.

"Can I take Shep to school?"

"Of course not, Wendy."

"Why not?" Wendy was stalling for time.

"Dogs don't go to school, Wendy."

"Can I take Shep out for a walk when I get home from school?" Wendy asked.

"Well, you can try, but I don't think he'll be able to walk on a leash yet."

Her mother put a plate of fried eggs in front of Wendy. She sat down in the chair next to Wendy and sipped her coffee.

"Darling," Wendy's mother asked softly. "Is there anything wrong at school?"

"Oh, no," said Wendy a little too loudly. "Everything's fine." She tried to smile happily. "Great!" she said. "Wonderful," she added.

Now she really sounded like a liar, but she couldn't stop.

"It's really so much fun in Miss Hunter's class. We're learning a lot this year. We're learning about families in different countries. We have this terrific book called *Families Around the World*. There's Manuel who lives in Spain and helps his father make guitars. There's Olav who lives in Norway — his family has a dairy farm and he has a pet goat. Now we are up to Jane who lives in a little thatched cottage in England and drinks tea all the time, even though she's only a kid. That's as far as we've got," Wendy finished. "Well, I guess I'll be going now."

"Wendy, you haven't started eating yet."

"Oh, I forgot." Wendy sat down again. She knew she was acting strange. Her mother was staring at her. Wendy began eating.

"Mom, can you pick me up at school today?"

Wendy's mother was trying to write a note to the teacher and didn't hear Wendy's question. She tore up the note she was working on and pulled out another piece of stationery. She licked her pencil and started again. Wendy thought her mother looked like a little kid.

She wrote very slowly, "Wendy wasn't feeling very well, but now she feels better . . ."

"That doesn't make sense," her

mother said, and tore up another piece of her good stationery.

"Mom?"

"Yes, Wendy."

"Can you pick me up at school today?"

"Why can't you walk? You know Friday is a bad day for me."

"I just feel sort of weak," said Wendy.

"Well, all right," her mother said. "Wait for me in front of the steps."

In front of the steps? That was where Stanley Kane hung out after school.

"I think I will walk home," said Wendy.

Her mother looked at her in a very strange way.

"Whatever you like." She shrugged. Then she wrote the note in a hurry.

Dear Miss Hunter,
Wendy didn't feel well this week. We decided to keep her home for a few days. Now she seems better.

Sincerely,
Dorothy Kent

"Well, I'm telling the truth, at least." Her mother stuck the note into the pocket of Wendy's school bag. "Bye, dear." She kissed Wendy.

When Wendy got to the corner of her block, she suddenly had the strangest feeling. It was almost as if she were outside of herself, watching herself walk to school. Her hands and feet turned cold and something inside her head started buzzing. Wendy stopped and sat down on the curb.

What was she doing? Today was Friday. That meant assembly and sitting next to Stanley Kane because they went in alphabetical order — Kane and Kent. Last week Stanley had spent the whole assembly period giving her hard jabs in the arm. Of course Miss Hunter didn't notice. Then there would be art class, recess, walking home — without Karen.

No. She couldn't go to school. But she couldn't play sick either — even if

she was really sick. She had used up that excuse.

Wendy sat on the curb. She kept telling herself, "Get up. You'll be late for school." But she couldn't move. Then she got an idea. It was a daring idea, not at all like Wendy.

Wendy had never played hookey in her life.

She got up and brushed off her skirt. She picked up her school bag. She

turned around and started walking back
home.

When she came to the hedge in front
of her house, she crouched down. Her
mother would probably be in the
kitchen, she thought. And from the
kitchen window her mother might see
her if she went through the yard to
the cellar door.

So Wendy crawled through the hedge
and ran across her mother's mint

garden. She flung herself flat against the side of her house. Then she inched along it very slowly. As she passed under the kitchen window, she heard her mother's voice. At first, she thought her mother was singing. Then she realized her mother was talking to Shep. When Wendy reached the cellar door, she pulled it open very quietly and let herself in. She was sure her mother hadn't heard.

Wendy tiptoed down the cellar stairs. It was dark and she wished she had her flashlight. An old couch draped with sheets suddenly loomed up in front of her.

Wendy felt her way along the wall until she reached the closet that was her secret War Room. There was a padlock on the door, but her mother never locked it. Wendy slipped off the lock and put it back on the hook. Then she crept into the closet.

The closet was pitch dark and the mothballs smelled more than Wendy remembered. It sure felt different without a flashlight — and without Karen to keep her company. She pulled the door closed behind her. (Karen always made her keep it open a crack.)

Wendy felt for her map with the push pins. Then she slid down on the floor and sat against the wall, her legs curled up under her.

Sitting It Out

Hours seemed to go by. The closet got hotter and hotter. Wendy was sweating. Could she last until three o'clock? Would she smother? The air in the closet was so stuffy, Wendy had trouble breathing. She thought about her classroom — so light and bright and cheery. And Miss Hunter was a nice teacher. Too bad she never seemed to notice what went on behind her back.

Wendy lost all track of time. She wondered how she would know when it was three o'clock. She didn't have a watch. Well, it certainly wasn't three o'clock, yet.

But, she thought, it's probably time for lunch.

Wendy felt around in her school bag and pulled out her sandwich. She was very hungry.

"Oh, no!" She smelled tunafish. She liked tunafish, but it was very messy and fell apart easily. It was especially hard to eat in the dark. Wendy had trouble finding her own mouth. A piece of tunafish and mayonnaise went down the front of her dress. It felt horrible. She was sure she was getting tunafish in her hair, too. She ate her apple and decided to save her cookies for later.

She hugged her knees. All she could smell was mothballs. Maybe she was smothering. She decided to open the door a little.

But, before she could open the door, she heard a noise. Something was rustling around in the closet. She froze and held her breath. "No, you're just dreaming," she told herself. "You must have dragged your school bag."

She waited. There *was* something in the closet with her. She was sure of it. She began to think of all the things it could be.

"A rat!" She suddenly remembered a picture on the cover of a horror comic. A bony man was tied up in a cave, and horrid gleaming red rat eyes stared out of the darkness.

But she had never heard her parents complain of rats in the basement.

Her father was worried about termites, however.

"It's a termite," she thought. But Wendy had no idea what a termite looked like. Her father said they could chew down a whole house.

"Don't think about it," she told herself. But she couldn't stop thinking.

If termites could eat a whole house, what could they do to a person? Wendy

wished she could look up termites in
her little picture dictionary. She wished
she at least knew what they looked like.

"Does a termite have claws?" she asked herself. Then she pictured a hairy little beast with big sharp claws.

"What kind of teeth does a termite have?"

"Big." Wendy answered her own question. If it could eat a whole house, it must have enormous teeth. Maybe even like a shark.

"What color eyes?"

"Red," she guessed and felt shivers going up and down her back.

Wendy sat in the dark and imagined the fierce hairy termites who were hiding out, watching every move she made. They were all around — in the bags of clothes, under her feet . . .

"This is too much. I'd rather face a real live bully any day."

Now she was getting carried away. "No," she told herself, "I'll just find a better hiding place. It's probably after two o'clock anyway."

Wendy crept to the door and started pushing it open. Then an amazing thing happened. The cellar was suddenly flooded with light.

Wendy heard her mother's voice. She was coming down the cellar steps and she was still talking to Shep.

"Be a good doggie and wait there," she called. "I think I can find you an old ball of Wendy's to play with."

Wendy pulled back into the closet.

"I know it's here," her mother muttered to herself, as she rummaged through Wendy's old toy chest.

"Hmm," she said. "Maybe I put it in a drawer."

When Wendy's mother passed the closet, she noticed that the door was open a crack. She pushed it shut and fixed the padlock. Wendy heard her fussing with the lock. Then she heard a click.

"Now, why did I do that?" Her

mother sounded fed up. "I don't even have the key."

Wendy suddenly heard a strange voice in her head. It was talking in a very reasonable voice — very calm and very quiet, almost like Miss Hunter.

"Wendy," it said, "you are locked in the closet.

"Wendy," it continued, "there is a good chance you will be here forever."

Wendy's mother suddenly heard the most blood-curdling scream she had ever heard in her life.

"Ma-a-a-a-a . . ." it wailed.

Back to School

When Wendy finally got out of the closet, it was exactly 10:30 A.M.

There were tools all over the place. Her mother had been forced to take the whole lock off the door. Her mother's face was dirty and her hair was a mess.

Worst of all, her mother was sobbing. Wendy had only seen her mother cry once in her whole life.

"How could you, Wendy?" Mrs. Kent sniffed and pushed her hair back. Then her face changed. She looked angry.

"What's the matter with you, anyway?" She grabbed Wendy's arm and marched her upstairs. Wendy was glad her mother never thought of looking in the closet. What if she had seen the Bully Map? How could she explain that?

"Change your clothes immediately. You have tunafish all over." Her mother was talking through clenched teeth.

"You're going right to school."

Wendy went upstairs. She washed the tunafish out of her ears. She brushed it out of her hair as best she could. She changed into her pink blouse and black jumper with red cherries on the pocket. She still smelled of tunafish, but she couldn't keep her mother waiting. She had never seen her mother so mad.

In a few minutes she was downstairs.

Her mother didn't offer to make another lunch, and Wendy was afraid to ask. Shep seemed to know something was wrong. He kept licking her ankles.

Her mother hurried her into the car.

When they arrived at school, it was only 11:30. Her mother was no longer crying; she wasn't talking either. She took Wendy to the principal's office and got her a late pass.

Wendy had missed assembly, but she was just in time for art class. Her mother walked her to the door of the art room and said, "I'll pick you up today in front of the school. We're going to have a little talk."

When Wendy walked in the door, everyone stopped painting and looked at her.

The first surprise was Stanley Kane. He was looking at her almost admiringly.

"You're late," he whispered. "Betcha you're in a whole lot of trouble."

Wendy gave a slight nod. It was funny that a bully could only respect you when he thought you had done something wrong. If Stanley knew she had tried to play hookey, he would really be impressed. He thought she was such a goody-goody.

Wendy put a piece of paper on her easel and began a new painting. She wanted to do a portrait of Shep. She started a big painting of Shep's face.

Stanley left her alone. He was busy picking on Roger, a short boy with huge glasses, who was painting on the other side of him. Roger was the smallest boy in the class.

When Mrs. Dover came by, she didn't say, "Ver-r-r-y nice," as she often did. She said, "Why, Wendy, that's just wonderful."

"I got a dog for my birthday," said Wendy shyly. "His name is Shep."

"Oh," said Monica, who had her easel on the other side of Wendy. After Mrs. Dover had gone, Monica leaned over and whispered,

"Can I see your dog sometime?"

"Sure," whispered Wendy, "but I'm not allowed to bring him to school." She was going to invite Monica to her house right then, but decided not to — not yet, anyway. She didn't really know Monica very well. Monica was new this year.

Wendy had never done a better painting. Shep looked just like Shep.

Wendy went to the supply cabinet to find a smaller brush. Then she realized what she was doing.

She ran back to her easel. On the way she tripped over Monica's easel and the whole thing collapsed on the floor. There was paint all over the place and all over Monica.

"Wendy," said Mrs. Dover. "Get some paper towels and take Monica to the girls' room to help her get cleaned up."

Wendy and Monica went to the girls' room.

"Oh, Monica, I'm so sorry," Wendy kept saying.

"That's okay," said Monica. "I didn't like my painting anyway."

When they finished cleaning up Monica, Wendy went back to her easel.

She wasn't the least bit surprised to see that Shep had a black beard and mustache.

She turned to Stanley Kane who was

busy giving Roger little sharp jabs in the arm. Roger's face was red and all bunched up. Behind his thick glasses, his eyes were screwed up.

Wendy knew Roger was trying not to cry. Wendy thought her painting looked bad, but Roger's looked worse. Splatters of black paint were all over his painting of a farmhouse.

"Leave him alone, Stanley," said Wendy. Was that really her voice? It sounded so loud and sharp.

Stanley was so taken aback, he stopped tormenting Roger for a minute.

"Mind your own business," he whispered furiously.

"What's going on over there?" asked Mrs. Dover. But, before she could come over, things happened very fast.

Wendy swung her foot at the legs of Stanley's easel, and the easel toppled over onto Stanley. Stanley was covered from head to toe with yellow paint.

The class started to laugh. Stanley was in a rage. For a moment, Wendy thought he was going to punch her, but instead he turned to Roger and pulled Roger's eyeglasses off.

Then came the biggest surprise of all. Roger swung his fist blindly and it connected hard with Stanley's nose.

Stanley put his hand up to his nose and then looked at it. His hand was covered with blood. He stared at the blood and then let out a loud howl. Then he started to blubber like a baby. He threw Roger's glasses on the floor and began jumping up and down on them, until they broke into little pieces. Stanley screamed and cried the whole time.

Everyone started talking at once. No one could believe what had happened. Mrs. Dover kept clapping her hands.

"Class, class . . ."

No one paid any attention. Mrs.

Dover went to the light switch and began flipping it on and off.

When everyone finally quieted down, Mrs. Dover said, "Mark, take Stanley to the nurse."

Stanley was still bawling when he left the room.

"Roger, I am surprised at you!" Mrs. Dover was staring at Roger, shocked.

"It wasn't his fault," Wendy heard herself say.

Roger turned sharply to Wendy.

"Be quiet," he muttered.

He turned and faced Mrs. Dover.

"It was my fault!" he said proudly.

Then he just stood there, grinning and blinking his eyes.

Monica

"Well, you never can tell," Wendy said to Monica. They were sitting in the school cafeteria. Monica shared her peanut butter and bacon sandwich with Wendy, because Wendy had no lunch.

"He's a monster," Monica said. They were talking about Stanley Kane, naturally.

"I'm sorry he ruined your picture of Shep. It was the best picture I ever saw."

Both girls looked over to the table where Roger was sitting, surrounded by kids. Roger had become a hero. He looked embarrassed by all the attention he was getting. His mother had brought another pair of glasses to school, so he sat there blinking at his sandwich and taking a nibble now and then.

Monica had hundreds of questions about Shep. Her mother wouldn't let her have a dog. Her mother said she had enough problems. (Monica had four brothers.)

When Wendy told her how Shep arrived on a pink satin pillow in a little basket, Monica kept nodding at every word. Wendy wasn't allowed to leave out anything.

"What does Shep eat?" Monica asked. "What does he look like when he's asleep? Can he do any tricks?"

Wendy loved talking about Shep.

"Maybe you could come over on Sunday and meet Shep," said Wendy. She was feeling more and more friendly toward Monica.

Then Wendy remembered that her

mother might have some punishment in store for her.

"I'll have to ask my mother, I guess," Wendy sighed. "I'm in a little bit of trouble."

They wrote down each other's phone numbers. Wendy decided Monica was a very nice person. She wished Monica walked home from school, but one of her older brothers picked her up every day.

To Wendy's surprise, Karen was at school. She was sitting alone at a table in the back of the cafeteria. When Wendy saw her, she knew right away why Karen was sitting all by herself.

Karen looked awful. Her face was swollen and one eye was higher than the other. There were blotches of pink all over her face.

Karen was looking down at her food. She looked lonely and sad.

"Excuse me," Wendy said to Monica.

She went over to Karen's table. Wendy saw that Karen's arms were swollen and blotchy, too.

"Hi," she said to Karen. Wendy sat down and tried to pretend that everything was normal.

Karen didn't look up.

"I was sick, too," said Wendy.

Karen still didn't say anything.

"Well, to tell the truth — I wasn't all that sick."

Karen didn't seem interested in anything. Wendy kept trying. "You'll never guess what I got for my birthday."

Then she noticed that Karen was holding her nose.

"Why are you doing that?"

"Tunafish," mumbled Karen. "I smell tunafish."

"Oh, that's me," said Wendy, feeling a little hurt.

"Allergic," said Karen and she started fanning at the air with her other hand.

Wendy thought Karen was being silly! Karen couldn't get a rash from a smell. Wendy wondered if she should move away. The children at a nearby table were beginning to look at her and Karen.

"Sitting with someone who is holding her nose isn't very good for my reputation," thought Wendy. But then she thought how awful Karen must feel, and she decided to stick it out. After all, Karen was her best friend.

"Will you walk home with me after school?"

As soon as she asked, Wendy remembered that her mother was picking her up.

"Can't," said Karen, still holding her nose.

"What about Sunday? Can you come over on Sunday? It's my real birthday. Then I could show you what I got. It'll be a surprise."

"Maybe I will . . ." said Karen. She took her fingers off her nose for a second and took a deep breath. Then she held her nose again.

". . . and maybe I won't . . ." finished Karen.

Wendy was beginning to feel that Karen had some nerve holding her nose like that. Especially since Wendy was being nice to admit she even knew such a freak. No one else was talking to Karen. In fact, they were trying not to stare at her. Every once in a while someone would look over at Karen and then turn back and whisper to somebody else.

Wendy left the table and went back to sit with Monica. Karen was watching her. When Karen saw her sit down again with Monica, she tossed her head, stuck her nose in the air, and gave a big sniff.

Wendy thought what a strange morning this had been.

More Surprises

That afternoon wasn't what Wendy expected either.

When Stanley Kane came back from the nurse's office, he was a little quieter than usual, but not much.

"You'll be sorry," he whined at Wendy. Wendy knew he blamed her for everything that had happened in art class. "I'll get you."

When they walked in line to music class, Stanley walked behind her and stepped on her heels. Her shoes kept coming off, and she had to keep stopping to pull them on again.

Things hadn't changed much; the

only difference was that Wendy just didn't feel so bad. Monica smiled at her every time she caught her eye, and Wendy hoped like anything that her mother would let her have a little birthday party on Sunday.

Then, during the last period, Miss Hunter made an announcement that made Wendy forget everything else.

"This year the PTA wants the third grade to help in the sale of raffle tickets for the Annual Carnival."

Everyone began to clap, except Wendy.

Miss Hunter went on.

"But first you need permission from your parents to sell tickets."

Wendy tried to imagine herself walking around the neighborhood knocking on doors. She thought about her Bully Map. There wasn't one street near her that didn't have a TYPE A or a TYPE B Bully on it. She pictured the orange and red push pins. Wendy decided that she would just tell Miss Hunter that her parents wouldn't give her permission.

Miss Hunter was still talking. "Now, I want your suggestions as to how the class will organize the sale of tickets."

"The person who sells the most tickets gets a prize," suggested Larry.

"The PTA is already offering a prize to the person who sells the most tickets," Miss Hunter said.

"Ha!" said Larry. "I'll bet my father will buy a hundred tickets."

Everyone groaned and looked at each other. Larry's father was rich. He would have a head start.

Wendy looked around the room. Everyone seemed to be giving up.

Jane raised her hand.

"I think it should be a rule that no one can sell more than two tickets to his or her own family."

"But," said Miss Hunter. "The whole idea is to sell as many tickets as possible. Each ticket costs 50 cents, so the more tickets sold, the more money for the school."

"I think we should work in teams," said Monica.

Suddenly Wendy felt a slight hope. If she were going around with someone else, it might not be so scary — especially if that person were Monica.

But then she thought of the Bully Map again.

Larry was talking again. "If we go in teams, no one will know who sold the most tickets and wins the prize."

"That's true," Miss Hunter agreed.

The discussion was making Wendy mad. All anyone seemed to care about was winning the prize. Wendy was so fed up, she almost raised her hand. But then, even the idea of talking aloud in class made her face burn and her throat get dry. She changed her mind. She wasn't even going to sell tickets, anyway.

The bell rang. School was over for the day.

"I want everyone to think about this over the weekend," said Miss Hunter.

Miss Hunter began sniffing the air.

"I smell tunafish," she said. She went to the coat closet and began sniffing there.

"Did someone leave an old sandwich here?"

Wendy left the classroom as quickly as she could.

Nasty Neil, Horrible Hilda, and Big Eddie

"Where were you?" Wendy's mother asked when she picked her up. "I told you to wait outside the school."

Wendy had been hiding inside the school door, waiting for her mother.

"I almost drove off when I didn't see you," her mother said crossly. Then she was quiet as they drove the rest of the way home.

"Come in the kitchen. I want to talk to you." Mrs. Kent pushed open the front door.

Wendy dragged her feet into the kitchen. She wondered how she was going to be punished. It didn't seem fair. Wendy felt it was years ago that she had hidden in the closet.

"Sit down." Wendy put her school bag on the table and sat down. Her mother put away a few groceries. Then she sat down, too.

The house was quiet — too quiet.

"Where's Shep?" asked Wendy. Her mother didn't answer. Wendy jumped up.

"Ma —" She pushed her chair back and ran to the pantry. Shep wasn't anywhere to be seen.

Wendy began to cry.

"How could you? It wasn't my fault. How could you give Shep back? You don't understand anything. I just couldn't go to school."

Wendy was sobbing so hard, she could hardly talk. "Shep — Shep —"

Her mother was standing behind her. She put a hand on Wendy's shoulder.

"Wendy —"

Wendy pulled away and turned to face her mother. She could hardly see through the tears.

"You gave Shep back," Wendy screamed. "I hate you. How would you like it? How would you like facing Stanley Kane every day and you finally get home in one piece and your mother is the worst of all."

"Wendy," her mother said sharply. "Shep's outside. I put him on a chain in the backyard."

Wendy ran out the back door. Sure enough. There was Shep, happily chewing on an old ball. When he saw her, he jumped up and tried to run to her, but the chain held him back.

"Oh, Shep, you were missing." Wendy picked him up. He was wiggling so much, Wendy was afraid he was going to slip out of her arms. He licked her face and hair.

"Oh, Shep."

Wendy's mother was at the door.

"You can play with Shep later, Wendy. Come on. We've got to get this over with."

Wendy and her mother sat down at the kitchen table again. Mrs. Kent handed Wendy a paper napkin to wipe her eyes.

"Wendy, I wouldn't give Shep away."

"I thought you were punishing me for playing hookey from school."

"Wendy, I was angry this morning. I was angry because I was confused and sad. I know something has been the matter ever since school began. Don't you want to talk about it?"

"Not really," Wendy said. But she wished she could talk about it.

"Let me know if you change your mind." Her mother got up. Wendy was afraid she was going to leave her.

"Mom," she said.

"What, dear?" Her mother came back.

"I don't hate you."

Wendy's mother laughed. "I know you don't. I just knew something was wrong and I guessed that it was either trouble with friends, work, or someone you are scared of."

When her mother said, "someone you are scared of," Wendy looked up.

"I know what it feels like," her mother said gently, putting her hand on top of Wendy's head. Then she said, "What does this Stanley Kane do, anyway?"

"Oh, things," said Wendy.

"Wendy, did I ever tell you about Nasty Neil?"

"Nasty Neil?" She stared at her mother. Then she laughed. "Who's that?"

"Nasty Neil was a bully who lived up the street. He had it in for me."

"What would he do?" asked Wendy.

"Terrible things — mean things."

"Like what?" Wendy tried to think of

her mother as a little kid.

Now her mother seemed shy about talking.

"C'mon, Mom."

"Well, his favorite trick was taking my school bag and throwing it over a high hedge. Then I would have to crawl through and get it back. It made me late for school every day and by the time I got to school, I was a mess."

"He did that every day?" asked Wendy. Her mother nodded.

"Well, why didn't you tell someone?" asked Wendy.

Then she and her mother realized what Wendy said, and they both started to laugh.

"What else did he do?" asked Wendy.

"Oh, taking things — like my ice cream money. But he was nothing compared to Hilda the Horrible!"

"Hilda the Horrible?" breathed Wendy.

When her mother ran out of stories, Wendy told her a few of the things Stanley did to her and to the other kids.

"What I'd like to do to him," her mother kept saying, just like Karen. Wendy was happy that her mother did not offer to call Stanley's mother. And it was interesting to Wendy that her mother didn't have more answers to the Bully Problem than Wendy did.

Then Wendy told her about Roger punching Stanley in art class that morning. Wendy's mother really enjoyed *that* story.

They were still talking when Wendy's father came home. He listened for a while. Then he joined in.

"You think you have problems?" He was sitting with them at the kitchen table. "I went to school in the toughest part of the city. But my mother never let me dress like the other kids. I was always dressed up in these fancy clothes — you know — a suit and tie. She made me polish my shoes every morning."

"Well?" said Wendy.

"Well, at the corner of my block this kid, Big Eddie, waited for me every day. Every day he blocked my way, grabbed me by the tie and said, 'Where d'ya think you're going, kid?'"

Wendy looked at her father. When he talked about Big Eddie, he really looked scared.

"Now, Big Eddie didn't just tease me about my clothes, like the other kids did. He punched me, he kicked me, he threw rocks at me, until one day . . ."

"What happened?" Wendy leaned forward.

"Well," her father began slowly. "I don't know exactly what happened. I guess I just went wild. I completely lost my head. I started punching Big Eddie as hard as I could. And once I started I couldn't stop. Even when his father came by on his way home from work, I was still hitting him. His father started pulling Big Eddie home, but I was following him, screaming and hitting him over and over."

Her father laughed. "You should have seen how embarrassed Big Eddie's father was. He kept waving me back and muttering, 'Go away, kid. Leave us alone, kid.' Then he would pass someone he knew and tip his straw hat. And I followed them all the way home, punching Big Eddie, who was yelling bloody murder."

Wendy was giggling. Her father looked at her.

"You know, he never bothered me again."

"I could never do that," said Wendy. "I could never punch someone bigger than me."

"No," her father said thoughtfully.

"That might not be such a good idea. I wish I knew what to tell you."

"That's all right," said Wendy, and she felt very happy — happier than she had felt for weeks.

Party Plans

They were so busy talking, Wendy forgot all about her birthday party until the telephone rang.

Wendy's mother answered it and came back.

"It's for you, Wendy — it's a little girl — someone I don't know, named Monica."

"Oh, Mom," whispered Wendy. "I forgot to ask you if I could invite her and Karen to a little birthday party for me this Sunday. It could also be an introduction party for Shep."

"Sounds like a nice idea," her mother said.

"Oh, boy," said Wendy, and she ran to the phone.

"Hi." Monica sounded very shy on the phone.

"Hi," said Wendy.

There was a long pause.

"Oh," said Wendy. "I want to invite you to my birthday party on Sunday."

"I'll ask my mother," said Monica.

When she came back on the line, she said, "It's okay. My mother wants to talk to your mother."

Wendy got her mother and stood by happily while her mother told Monica's mother where they lived.

"Three o'clock would be fine," Wendy's mother said.

"Don't hang up. Don't hang up," whispered Wendy. "Let me talk to Monica again."

Then Wendy and Monica got back on the phone. They stayed on for a long time. When they couldn't think of anything more to say, they just giggled.

Neither one wanted to hang up.

An hour later Wendy's mother came into the room and saw Wendy sitting on the floor with Shep on her lap. Shep was chewing the earpiece of the telephone. Wendy had put Shep on the phone so that Monica could hear him pant.

"Hello, Shep," Monica's voice was saying at the other end.

"That's enough," Wendy's mother said.

"Well, I guess I have to go," said Wendy.

"Bye," said Monica. "See you Sunday."

Wendy called Karen to invite her to the party.

"Who else is coming?" asked Karen.

"Just you and Monica," said Wendy.

"I don't like her," said Karen, and she hung up.

Wendy felt terrible. She was about to tell her mother that Karen wasn't coming when the phone rang again.

Wendy picked up the phone. "Hello?"

"Hi." It was Karen.

Wendy waited.

"I'm allergic to chocolate cake," said Karen.

"I know," said Wendy. "We'll have lemon cake."

"Well, I guess I'll come," said Karen.

There was a long pause.

"Who's Monica, anyway?" asked Karen.

"You know who she is. She has short blond curly hair."

"The one you were sitting next to in the cafeteria?"

"That's her," said Wendy.

"Well — okay," said Karen.

When Wendy got off the phone, she wondered if she should have warned Karen about Shep. She knew Karen was afraid of all animals, but Wendy was sure Karen couldn't help but love Shep.

Sometimes Karen drove her crazy.

Shep Goes for a Walk

There was a lot to do Saturday morning. Wendy and her mother went shopping. Wendy picked out party favors for Karen, Monica, and Shep. They all got the same thing — a furry gray mouse that squeaked.

"For chewing up — or putting on your shelf to look at," said Wendy, "depending on who you are."

Then she and her mother decided that the lemon cake should have white icing with yellow and blue trim. They bought food coloring, flour, and lemons.

They stopped at another store and bought a big red satin bow for Shep.

When they got home, Wendy asked her mother if she could take Shep out for a walk on a leash.

"Well, you can try," her mother said.

But Shep didn't catch on to the idea of walking on a leash. He chewed on the leash. Then he ran in circles, winding the leash around Wendy's legs until her feet were tied together. She had to jump around in circles to get undone.

Then she got a better idea. She picked up Shep and went to the garage where she found her old doll carriage. She wheeled it into the driveway and put Shep inside, tying the leash to the metal bars on the side of the carriage.

Shep sniffed all around the carriage.

"Wait here." Wendy ran inside and got the new red bow.

"What are you up to, Wendy?" Her mother followed her outside and watched while Wendy tied the bow around Shep's neck. She shrugged and went back inside.

"Ready to go?" Wendy asked Shep.

As soon as she pushed the carriage, Shep fell over. That scared him and he crawled under the blanket and hid there until Wendy reached the corner of her block.

Shep peeked out. Wendy crossed the street. Now Shep was watching the scenery go by.

It was a beautiful autumn day. Wendy was having so much fun explaining the neighborhood to Shep, she was on her way to Karen's house before she knew it.

"Maybe I'll surprise Karen," thought Wendy. "Maybe I'll give her a sneak preview."

She turned into Karen's block.

"This is where my best friend, Karen, lives." Shep had his paws on the hood of the carriage. He seemed interested in everything. His ears were flying behind him and his tongue was hanging out.

"Yip," he barked at a tree.

"And this is where mean old Pat Haggerty lives," said Wendy cheerfully.

"It sure is," someone said.

Wendy looked up. It was mean old Pat Haggerty.

Pat Haggerty was standing right in front of the carriage, her legs wide apart, her hands on her hips.

Pat pointed at Shep. "What in the world is that?" She screeched with laughter. "That is ridiculous."

Shep was wagging his tail and trying to jump up to lick Pat.

"That's my dog," said Wendy as calmly as she could.

"You call that a dog?" Pat poked Shep.

A page from Wendy's Bully Log Book flashed into her head:

Bully type : A
Weight : 100 pounds
(mabye more)

Haggerty, Pat
Age: 10½years
Height: 4 Feet 9

Description : Piggy eyes, short
yellow hair, fat Pink face.
Habits : Kicking, throwing stones
rideing bikes in to you. and so on.
(see INCIDENTS SECTION. Pages
8, 10, 16, 18, 21, 25, and 27)

PLAN OF ACTION
Use Secret Plan 3,300. Code 3.

"Secret Plan 3300, Code 3" meant "Run!"

Wendy tried to turn the carriage around, but Pat was holding onto it, shaking it up and down. Shep slipped and rolled around.

"That's the stupidest thing I ever saw," said Pat, shaking the carriage even harder. "Little Rat Kid and her Little Rat Dog."

"Let go," said Wendy. She tried to stop the carriage from jiggling so much. Shep was being tossed all over the place.

"Give me that," said Pat. She grabbed the handle and gave Wendy a hard push. Wendy fell into the grass.

"I'll give him a good ride." Pat began pushing the carriage down the street. She began running with it.

"Let go of it!" screamed Wendy.

"You want me to let go?" called Pat. "Okay." And she let go.

The carriage took off by itself down a hill.

Wendy jumped to her feet and began chasing the carriage.

But Pat got there first and grabbed it. The carriage stopped, but Shep kept going. He tumbled out of the carriage and hung there, dangling from his leash.

Both girls stared in horror.

"He'll choke to death," Wendy heard Pat gasp. They both ran.

Wendy ran to Shep and picked him up. She held him close. His heart was beating very fast — and so was Wendy's. Wendy was sobbing. Shep was all right, but he was scared. He climbed up Wendy's shoulder and hid in her hair.

"Are you all right?" Wendy kept asking Shep.

"Are you all right?" mimicked Pat. But she had a funny look on her face. She looked scared and miserable. After a minute, she said, "Let me see." Pat reached out to touch Shep.

"Go away," said Wendy, pulling back.

"I have a right," said Pat Haggerty. "It's my block." But she didn't look sure of herself at all.

Wendy looked Pat right in the eye.

"I've had it, Pat Haggerty." Wendy heard herself talking in a cold, low voice. "I've really had it with you. It's one thing to torment people. It's another thing to hurt a helpless animal. This dog never did anything to you, and if you come one step closer, I'll . . ."

Wendy could not think of what she would do, but she sounded so sensible, she decided to go on.

". . . I'll . . . I'll tell you the truth about yourself. You're not just a bully. You're a TYPE A Bully."

"What's that?" asked Pat, looking scared, but interested.

"That's for me to know and you to find out." Wendy had to finish her speech some way. She didn't want to tell Pat that a TYPE A Bully was a dangerous person. Pat might be proud of that.

Wendy turned around and began walking home, carrying Shep in her arms. She was halfway up the block when Pat caught up to her. Pat was pushing the doll carriage in front of her.

"Don't you want this?" asked Pat.

Wendy kept walking.

"Listen, kid. . . ," said Pat, grabbing Wendy's arm.

Wendy tried not to look scared. She pulled away and walked faster. Pat ran alongside.

"I didn't mean to hurt the mutt," she said.

Wendy didn't say anything. Pat pushed the carriage in front of Wendy and blocked her way.

Wendy stopped. She looked at Pat. She didn't feel scared anymore. It seemed to her that there wasn't anything worse Pat could do than what she had already done. Besides, Pat still looked scared. Shep was still shaking. Pat noticed.

"I didn't mean to scare him," said Pat.

"I just thought I'd take him for a ride."

Wendy didn't say anything.

Pat pulled the carriage back and let Wendy pass. She followed Wendy until Wendy reached the traffic light at the corner. Pat put her hand on Wendy's shoulder. Wendy had to wait for the light to change. She was trapped. She turned and faced Pat.

"What now?" Wendy said.

"I had a dog once," said Pat.

"So?"

"His name was Reggie," Pat said softly. "He was hit by a car."

Wendy tried to see if Pat was telling the truth. Maybe she was trying to get Wendy to feel sorry for her. But Pat looked as if she were going to cry. Wendy believed her.

"I'm sorry to hear that," said Wendy. And she really was sorry — sorry for Reggie and sorry for Pat.

The light changed. They crossed the

street, Pat dragging the doll carriage behind her.

When they reached the other side, Pat grabbed Wendy again and wouldn't let her move.

Wendy got all mixed up. She felt angry and scared and sorry for Pat all at the same time.

"Wait here," said Pat, giving Wendy a shake. "If you're not here when I come back, you'll really get it." Pat suddenly let go of Wendy and looked ashamed of herself.

"What I meant was. . . ," said Pat, looking at the ground, ". . . promise me you'll wait for me. I want to run home and get something."

"What?" asked Wendy.

Pat was almost shy now. "Well, I thought I'd get Reggie's collar. Your dog can wear it when he gets bigger." She looked up at Wendy. "Please wait."

"I promise to wait," said Wendy, and she did.

Ten minutes later Wendy saw Pat running back. She looked very angry — just like her old self.

"Uh-oh," said Wendy to Shep, but she waited.

Pat was so angry and in so much of a hurry, she almost got hit by a car when she crossed the street.

But Pat wasn't angry at Wendy.

"My stupid mother threw it out." Pat said a few horrible things about her mother. "I went looking for this collar — I kept it in a velvet case in my drawer — and I couldn't find it anywhere. So I asked my mother and she said, 'That old thing? I threw it out.'"

"How awful," said Wendy.

"It was the only thing I had left to remind me of Reggie."

"What was he like?" asked Wendy.

Before Wendy knew it, she and Pat and Shep were sitting on the grass talking about Reggie. Wendy began to feel like Monica listening to her talking about Shep. Pat told Wendy all the funny things Reggie used to do.

"Wait a minute," Wendy said. "I think I remember him. Was he a sort of spotted, black-and-white dog with one ear kind of chewed up?"

"That's him!" shrieked Pat. Wendy was afraid Pat was going to kiss her. Pat was so delighted someone remembered Reggie.

After a while, Wendy said, "Well, I have to go now."

"Oh," said Pat, looking sad. "You forgot to tell me your dog's name."

"Shep," said Wendy.

"Nice name," said Pat.

"Well, I have to go." Wendy started to get up.

"Can I pet him?" asked Pat.

"Of course," said Wendy. Shep walked over to Pat and climbed in her lap. He began licking Pat's face and biting her fingers.

Wendy watched them, thinking how glad she was that Shep was so friendly. She thought it was nice, in a way, that Shep didn't even know the difference between Bullies and Other People.

"Oh," sighed Pat happily as Shep chewed on the sleeve of her jacket. "Just what Reggie used to do."

The Birthday Party

Karen looked beautiful when she came up the walk Sunday afternoon. She was the first to arrive at the birthday party. She was wearing a green velvet coat and a green velvet dress with a white lace collar. Her shiny black braids were tied with green ribbons, and she was carrying a large, bulky present.

The rash on her face was all gone, and she smiled happily at Wendy when Wendy opened the door.

"Hi!" they both said at the same time.

"Here," said Karen, handing Wendy the present.

"Thanks." Wendy opened it while Karen took off her coat.

It was an enormous stuffed poodle.

"Like it?" asked Karen eagerly.

"Oh, yes," said Wendy. "But wait until you see my real present."

Now why had she said that? Karen looked so disappointed.

"I didn't mean that," Wendy said and ran to the pantry to get Shep.

She fixed his red satin bow and combed his ears with a tiny comb. He looked wonderful. Then she took her pink blanket and covered Shep so she could really surprise Karen.

"Guess what it is," said Wendy as she popped out into the hallway.

Karen stared at the pink bundle.

"A doll?" Suddenly she jumped back.

"It moved!" she cried.

"Of course," said Wendy, delighted. "Da dum!" And with that, she pulled off the pink blanket. She watched Karen's face, waiting for her to burst into a smile and say, "Oh, he's adorable."

But Karen didn't say, "Oh, he's adorable." Her face turned pale and the freckles stood out. She began trembling.

"Yikes!" she screamed. "Take it away!"

But Wendy was so sure Karen would change her mind, she stuffed Shep into Karen's face.

"Here, touch him. He won't hurt."

Karen looked like she had just met King Kong. She ran up the stairs.

"Leave me alone. I want to go home." Karen was crying hard.

"You scaredy-cat," said Wendy.

"You should talk," screamed Karen.

Wendy thought Karen was dumb to be scared of a tiny puppy, so she followed her up the stairs and grabbed her arm. Karen tried to pull away, but Wendy held onto her hard.

"You're being silly." Wendy tried to

pull Karen down the stairs. It was hard
to hold onto Shep. He was barking
furiously at Karen.

"Shh . . . Shep, you're scaring her."
Wendy grabbed Karen's wrist and tried

to make her pet Shep. Shep growled and looked as if he were going to snap Karen's hand off.

Karen got loose and ran up to the second floor. Then she ran all the way up the next flight of stairs to the attic. She was screaming the whole time.

By now, Wendy's mother and father were standing in the hall, but Wendy didn't notice them when she shouted after Karen: "You big baby!" She made a horrible face. "Bla-a-a-a — I'll get my grandmother after you."

Wendy turned and saw everyone staring at her. Her mother pushed past her and went up to talk to Karen.

"I want to go home," Karen kept screaming.

In a few minutes Wendy's mother came down the stairs.

"I'm going to put Shep out in the backyard on a chain."

"Oh, no, Mom," cried Wendy. "The party is for him, too."

"I'm sorry, Wendy, but you never told me Karen was afraid of dogs."

"She's afraid of everything," said Wendy with disgust.

Wendy and her mother took Shep into the yard and tied him to a big chain. He looked so small and harmless but, when they looked up, they saw Karen's horrified face at the attic window. She was still screaming.

"Poor child," said Wendy's mother. "We'd better let her go home."

Wendy walked Karen to the corner. Karen stopped trembling and seemed to feel much better, but she wouldn't go back to the party.

Wendy wanted to say something. She felt terrible about the things she had said to Karen and the way she had acted. She was almost as bad as Pat Haggerty or Stanley Kane.

"Am I a bully?" she wondered. Maybe she would have to put herself into the Bully Log Book.

"I'm sorry," she finally said. "I'm sorry for the way I acted."

Karen was feeling pretty cheerful now.

"It's not your fault," Karen said. "I'm sorry I'm so scared of dogs. I really wanted to come to your party."

They walked a little further.

"Can you walk home from school with me tomorrow?" asked Wendy.

"Sure," said Karen. "If we walk to my house first." Then she stopped. "Oh, I forgot, I have to go to the doctor tomorrow. What about Tuesday?"

"Fine," said Wendy, and the two girls smiled at each other.

Wendy got back to the house just in time to greet Monica.

Monica loved everything about the party — and she adored Shep.

"Oh, look at what he is doing," she kept saying. "Isn't he clever?"

The cake was beautiful. It was a white cake with yellow and blue roses and little green leaves. It was the perfect birthday cake until Shep fell into it.

Or rather — until Shep was dropped into it.

Wendy hadn't meant to drop Shep in the cake. Right after she blew out the candles, she and Monica thought Shep should get a chance to see the cake. So she picked him up to show him.

But Shep scrambled out of her hands. He stood in the middle of the cake and looked around at it. He sniffed a candle. Then he tried to get out. Everyone stared at the dog in the cake, wondering what to do.

Finally, Wendy's mother got some paper towels, wrapped them around Shep, and lifted him out of the cake. She tried to wipe off as much cake as she could, but Shep got away and hid behind the kitchen cabinet. He licked the rest of the cake off his fur. He really enjoyed it.

He was the only one who got to eat the birthday cake. Wendy's mother looked sadly at the cake which was all caved-in in the middle, with a few paw prints on the edges.

"I'm not fussy." Monica was looking longingly at a blue rose that hadn't been touched.

"Me neither," said Wendy.

But Wendy's mother said she didn't think it was a good idea to eat a cake that had a dog dropped into it. She went out to the bakery and brought back some delicious cupcakes.

Monica sighed as she ate her fourth cupcake. "This is the best party I've ever been to."

When Monica's mother came to pick

her up, she asked if Wendy could visit Monica the next Saturday.

"We don't have a dog," she said, admiring Shep. "But we have four cute boys."

"Ick," said Monica.

New Week at School

Karen and Monica finally got to meet each other at recess the next day. Wendy introduced them to each other and then sat back while Monica and Karen talked. It turned out that Karen knew a girl at the school Monica used to go to.

"What a stuck-up snob," said Monica.

"Boy, are you right!" said Karen.

Wendy felt very pleased.

There was a lot of noise on the other side of the school yard.

"What's that Stanley Kane up to now?" asked Monica. The three girls went over. There was already a crowd of kids standing around.

Stanley was standing over Roger, yelling at him. Every once in a while, he would shove Roger in the shoulder.

"What's going on?" Miss Hunter finally noticed something.

"I'm telling him to stay off my block," said Stanley. "No one can sell raffle tickets there but me."

"But I live on your block," said Roger.

"It's my territory," said Stanley, and he looked like he was going to punch Roger again.

"That's enough," said Miss Hunter. "We'll discuss the raffle sale this afternoon in class."

Wendy sat in the classroom, trying to figure out which route she should take home from school that afternoon. She had to walk by herself and she decided that walking behind the tennis courts might be scary if she were all alone.

She wasn't paying any attention to

the discussion of the raffle sale until she heard Christina saying, "It isn't fair. It isn't fair if we can only sell raffle tickets on our own block. Nobody lives on my block yet."

New houses were going up all around Christina's house.

"You come near my block and POW! You'll get it, just like that," said Stanley, glaring at Christina.

"Now Stanley," said Miss Hunter.

Roger's hand was up. "Besides, there are a lot of blocks where nobody in the class lives. Who will cover those blocks?"

"Good point," said Miss Hunter.

"Oh, who cares," said Larry. "I'm going to win the prize for the most tickets, anyway. My father could buy every ticket in the whole raffle if he wanted to."

Wendy looked at Larry. He was sitting back smugly. It was true, she thought. His father was the richest man in the community.

Before Wendy knew it, her own hand was up in the air.

"Why, Wendy," said Miss Hunter. "It's nice to hear from you."

Wendy's face was bright red. Everyone turned to look at her.

"I don't think trying to win the prize is a good idea," said Wendy slowly. "If what we really want to do is sell a lot of tickets, it would be better if the whole class cooperated. Maybe we could try to sell more tickets than the fourth grade — or even the sixth grade."

Miss Hunter was surprised. So was everyone else.

"What an interesting suggestion," said Miss Hunter. "Go on."

But Wendy couldn't go on. She had just talked more in class than she had for a whole year.

Monica's hand went up. "I agree with Wendy. Because, if everyone thinks Larry's going to win anyway, we'll all feel like giving up or maybe selling one or two tickets — and that's all."

"Hmm. . . ," said Miss Hunter. "But, if everyone is going to cooperate, we need organization. We need strategy."

"I don't like the whole thing," said Larry, and he glared at Wendy.

But Wendy didn't pay any attention to him. When Miss Hunter said the word "strategy" an idea began to form in the back of Wendy's mind.

She was an expert in strategy, wasn't she?

Wendy raised her hand again before she was even sure what it was she was going to say.

Miss Hunter was delighted. "Yes, Wendy."

"Well, we could have a big map of the whole neighborhood," she began, wondering what she was going to say next. "The first day everyone could sell wherever they wanted. We could work in teams," she added, looking at Monica.

"Then, the next day, everyone would come to class and mark on the map where they had sold raffle tickets. They could also mark down where people had said, 'No,' and where people had said, 'Come back later,' or where people weren't in or something — house by house. Then no one would repeat what anyone else had done."

"How could we mark all those things?" asked Miss Hunter.

Wendy was puzzled for a minute. Then the idea came to her. It was so simple.

"Push pins," she said.

"Push pins?"

"Well, yes," said Wendy. "For instance" — she was feeling braver and braver — "red, if you made a sale . . . uh . . . let's say, orange, if they said to come back later, and yellow for no!"

"I'm against that," called out Stanley, loudly.

Everyone turned around.

"It should be black for no," finished Stanley.

"Yellow," said Wendy.

"We will need a lot of push pins," said Miss Hunter.

"Well, it just so happens. . . ," said Wendy wondering if she were telling too much, "I just happen to have a supply. . . ."

She certainly did have a supply. Every week she spent her entire allowance on push pins. She had hundreds and hundreds of them and there were only twelve on the Bully Map. She almost giggled when she thought, "They would have to bring busloads of Bullies from all over the country and import Bullies from all over the world to use up all those push pins."

"Well, class," said Miss Hunter. "What do you think of Wendy's plan?"

Christina said, "I think it's very good. Every day we could study the map and decide on our strategy. We could see which blocks hadn't been covered. Then we could decide who should sell tickets there."

Roger added, "And if we saw an orange pin, meaning the people weren't home or said to come back later, then someone else could go back if it was easier for them."

Stanley was waving his hand wildly. Wendy didn't want to hear what Stanley was going to say now.

But Stanley sounded excited. "Is this map anything like a war map — like in a Command Post?"

Wendy turned around and faced Stanley. She looked him straight in the eye and said very sharply, "Exactly."

"Oh, boy!" said Stanley. "Miss Hunter, Miss Hunter, let's vote."

"I don't like the whole thing," said Larry again.

But, when they voted, everyone was in favor of Wendy's plan, except Larry.

"Well, that settles that," said Miss Hunter, looking pleased.

Roger raised his hand. "If we are going to be organized, we need a chairman and I elect Wendy."

"You mean you nominate Wendy," said Miss Hunter. "Not elect."

But Wendy *was* elected chairman of the raffle sale.

Everyone was excited.

"When can you be ready with the map?" asked Miss Hunter.

"Oh, tomorrow," said Wendy blushing terribly.

"So soon?" asked Miss Hunter.

Wendy walked home from school, planning her strategy for the raffle sale and thinking how she would have to make the map bigger to include the streets behind the school.

She wondered if she should dress differently — with pearls around her neck like a real chairman.

Then she thought about Karen and Monica making friends and wondered why that made her so happy. And Shep . . .

She was so busy thinking, she was almost home before she realized she had walked straight home from school . . . right through Bully Country.